LARRY LASER
FINDS HIS SPARK!

Written by
Cory Boone

Illustrated by
Jake Kimberlin

SPIE PRESS
Bellingham, Washington USA

Larry Laser was lonely and bored.

The only time anyone noticed him was when cats wanted to chase his laser spot.

"There has to be more out there for me!" Larry declared.

Larry knew life at home would never hold the excitement he was seeking, so he decided to go out and find his own adventure.

But what else might he be good at?

Larry tried baking, but his laser nose
burned everything to a crisp.

He tried acting, but it turned out Larry was much better at casting the spotlight than being in it.

He tried selling shoes, but the smell of feet made him sneeze. Even worse, every time he sneezed, he burned a hole in the shoes he was holding!

That evening, as Larry sat in the park feeding the birds, he wondered: was he better off as a cat toy?

As Larry watched all the happy people pass by him, a bird flew right into his face!

"Ahh! Get away from me!" Larry yelled, throwing the bread away from him.

Suddenly, Larry heard a loud crash. Someone walking by had slipped on the bread and fallen down!

"I'm so sorry!" Larry apologized.

"Are you OK?"

She looked up and smiled. "Don't worry.
I'm fine! I'm Lexi Lens by the way."

"I'm Larry. Larry Laser!"

"A laser?" Lexi said. "I've been looking for a laser to help me with a few things!
Any chance you're looking for a new job?"

THIS

WAY!

Larry shook his head sadly. "Oh, no. I think you're confused. Every time I try a new job, it ends terribly. My laser is just too strong."

Lexi smiled at Larry. "It sounds to me like you've been trying the wrong jobs. Come on, I know just what you need."

Lexi wasted no time in bringing Larry to meet Wally Welder.

Wally's job was to heat up different pieces of metal so that they would melt together. Wally was good at his job, but his welds were a little messy.

"Stand here and shine your laser," Lexi said.

Larry wasn't sure it was a good idea, but he did want to find a place to belong, so he did as Lexi asked.

To Larry's surprise, when his laser shone through Lexi's lens, it focused into a tiny spot on the metal. With Larry and Lexi's help, the pieces welded together faster and with less mess!

"That was amazing!" Larry said. "Can we do that again tomorrow?"

Lexi grinned. "Just wait," she replied. "We have some other adventures planned for tomorrow!"

The next day, Lexi brought Larry to the hospital and introduced him to Maria Mirror.

"Hi, Larry! Want to help out with some eye surgery and let people see better?"

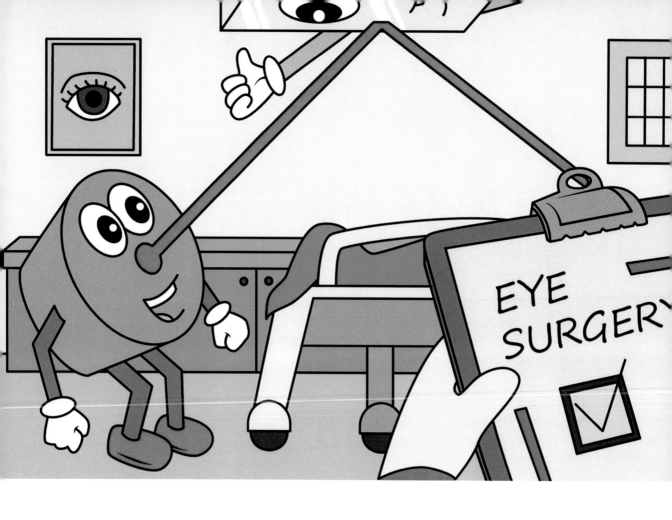

With Larry's laser reflecting off of Maria's mirror, the doctors could move the laser beam to change the shape of patients' eyes.

"Mr. Jones used to need really thick glasses," Lexi explained, "but now he can see without them!"

"I can!" Mr. Jones shouted. "I can see! Oh, thank you. Everything is so beautiful!"

ANOTHER ONE?!?!

Lexi smiled and turned to Larry.

"I have one more surprise for you tomorrow!" she told him.

Another surprise? Larry thought. *What could be better than this?*

The next day, Lexi introduced Larry to Frankie Fiber.

"Frankie sets up high-speed internet so everyone in their city can work, watch movies, and stay in touch with their families," Lexi explained.

"Hi, Larry!" said Frankie. "Lexi's right. It's my job to move information from one place to another. But to do so, I need to send laser pulses through a long fiber made of glass."

Larry's teeth chattered. The idea of the whole internet depending on him left him feeling nervous, but after his last few successes he was feeling more confident.

So, closing his eyes, he shone his light into Frankie. It worked!

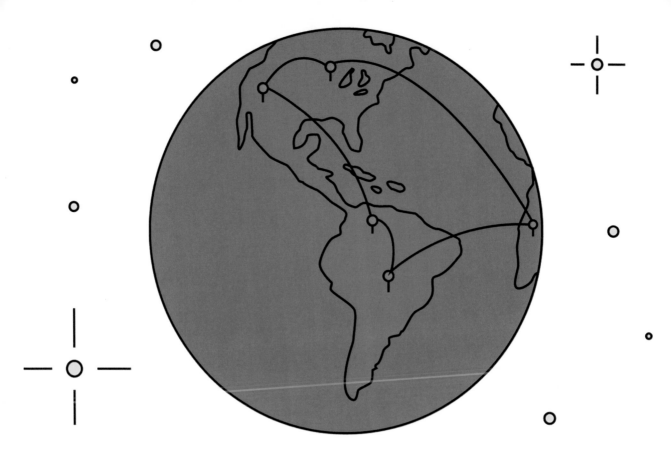

"Thanks a lot, you two!" said Frankie. "Did you know there are optical fibers going across the whole ocean, letting people stay connected all across the world?"

Larry hadn't known that. But suddenly, he felt less alone. He had helped connect people. Him!

HIGH

FIVE!

Outside, Lexi high-fived Larry.

"Great job this week! We couldn't have done any of it without you."

Larry smiled. Knowing he had helped people all week long felt great! But learning about all he could do felt even better.

"Thank you, Lexi, so much! But now it's my turn to show you something new."

Larry took Lexi back to his cats. "Whee!" Lexi cheered. "Look at them go!"

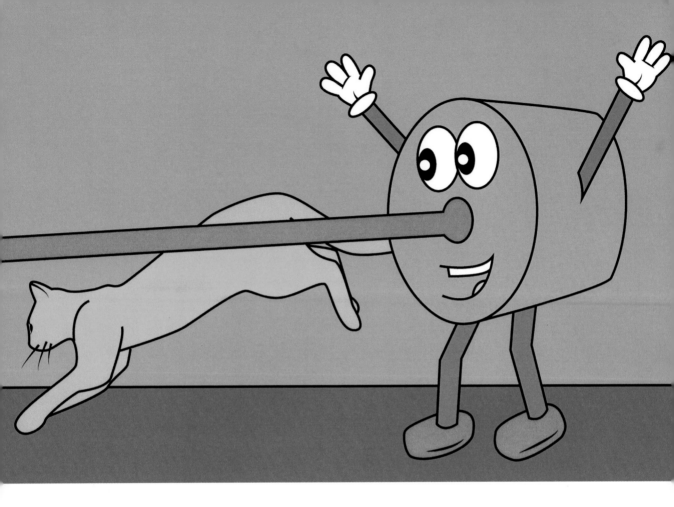

Larry laughed as he watched Lexi play with the cats. He'd forgotten just how much fun it could be to watch them run and play. But with Lexi by his side, everything seemed new again.

Larry grinned. He had learned that he was so much more than just a toy for the cats. And he couldn't wait to get out there and do it again.

But for right now, he was perfectly happy right where he was.